Thomas Cyprian Williams

Lyrics of Lincoln's Inn

With Notes for the Benefit of the Unlearned

Thomas Cyprian Williams

Lyrics of Lincoln's Inn
With Notes for the Benefit of the Unlearned

ISBN/EAN: 9783744770927

Printed in Europe, USA, Canada, Australia, Japan

Cover: Foto ©Andreas Hilbeck / pixelio.de

More available books at **www.hansebooks.com**

LYRICS OF LINCOLN'S INN,

WITH NOTES FOR THE BENEFIT OF THE UNLEARNED.

BY

T. CYPRIAN WILLIAMS,

OF LINCOLN'S INN, BARRISTER-AT-LAW, LL.B.

London:

SWEET AND MAXWELL, LIMITED,

3, CHANCERY LANE, W.C.

—

1896

PREFACE.

"THE Bitter Cry of the Upright Trustee," and most of the other pieces here collected (Nos. 3—6 and 8—12), were published anonymously in the *St. James's Gazette* between 1888 and 1892, and they are now reprinted by the kind permission of the proprietors, to whom the writer's best thanks are due. *Lord Ailesbury and Lord Iveagh's case* appeared in the *Law Times*. The rest of the verses are printed for the first time.

The picture on the cover is reproduced from a drawing by Mrs. CYPRIAN WILLIAMS.

TABLE OF CONTENTS.

Dedication

To the Student of Law.

I have often addressed thee in grave dissertation ;
    I have penned for thee many a solemn discourse ;
I have toiled to encompass thy edification,
    An end which is rarely effected by force !

I should hardly surmise thou hast blessed me, thy teacher
    On subjects admittedly dry and abstruse.
Hast thou bade me go hang for a long-winded preacher,
    Perhaps thou art not without valid excuse !

For light-hearted youth is impatient of labour.
    Alas ! that its joyousness ever should end !
We may all fling an innocent curse at our neighbour,
    And none the less give him regard as a friend.

Thou art dear to my heart as the child to the nurse's !
    I would have thee make merry, for life is not long.
So to thee will I offer this garland of verses,
    Where law is enlivened with jest and with song.

And I drink to thy courage !   For as I grow older,
    And study the intricate maze we are in,
The vastness of law so appals the beholder,
    That I honour the youth who has pluck to begin !

The Bitter Cry of the Upright Trustee.

Lives there a man too good to have reflected with disgust,
How bare a thing is ownership, when clothèd with a trust?

What profit to have lands and goods possessed for others' use?
A thankless task to hold the rind, while others suck the juice.

A promise to do work, not asking pay or satisfaction,
Ranks as a naked compact, and is not a cause of action.[1]

But to accept a trust involves a legal obligation,
Though naught be given in return, as a consideration.[2]

For should I, jointly or alone, take goods on trust for thee,
The benefit is thine, and oh! the detriment to me!

---

[1] *Ex nudo pacto non oritur actio.* In English law a naked agreement is one whereby the promisor receiveth no benefit, nor doth the promisee incur any detriment in consideration of the promise. And this is at the common law.

[2] And this is in equity. For equity, as Lord Bacon hath said, looketh beyond the common law to the corrupt conscience of him that will deal with the land he holds in trust, knowing it in equity to be another's.

My hard position only finds disfavour with the Court.[3]
I risk its pitiless decree, if I should fail in aught.

And at my peril I must rule my actions (if I can)
As ordereth his own affairs the prudent business man.[4]

The prudent business man "that never was on land or sea,"
But yet exists[5] to shame us as an abstract entity !

And what he doth for profit, that must I without reward ;
No payment for my services doth equity accord.[6]

It lays a galling burthen on the conscience of the just,
The duty of administering property in trust.

How doth the fraudulent trustee contrive an easy gain ?
He realizes all the funds, then goes to live in Spain.[7]

He leaves his *c. q. t.*[8] to writhe in impotent affliction,
And cynically takes his ease beyond the jurisdiction.

---

[3] "Trustees are invariably made joint tenants."   "Joint tenancy is not favoured in equity."   See the Text-Books.

[4] The general rule of equity is that trustees should administer their trust property with the same care that a prudent man of business exercises in administering his own affairs.

[5] *Scilicet* (with much else), in the contemplation of equity only.

[6] The rule of equity is, that a trustee shall make no profit by his trust.

[7] Spain, the common refuge of gentlemen in trouble ; there was long no extradition treaty between England and Spain.

[8] *Cestui que trust*, the technical term for one, in trust for whom another holds property.

Why do not I escape, like he, to affluence abroad ?
It is because I am too altruistic to defraud.

But why should he be conscienceless, and I be altruistic ?
The forces which have cast our minds in different moulds are mystic.

And mine's of that peculiar cast which scorns dishonest profit,
So I remain a bare[9] trustee.   And "that's the humour of it."

To other people's business I give trouble, toil and time,
And do not rob them, but express my discontent in rhyme.

---

[9] The reason why one is said to be a *bare* trustee lieth mainly in this, that such an one hath no beneficial interest in the property he holdeth on trust.

The Married Women's Property Act (1882),
partly Re-drawn.
(1888.)

There's a pleasurable fancy fostered by a recent Act,[1]
That the law enables every married woman to contract :

And a superficial student might incautiously conclude
That all wives who buy on credit can successfully be sued.

But 'tis not an easy enterprise to prove a wife a debtor ;
For the spirit killeth tradesmen's hopes of payment (not the letter).

Hear the meaning of the statute, which its words at first concealed,
Now by manifold decision at a vast expense revealed !

You may sue a married woman for the price of goods supplied ;
But 'twixt suing and recovering the difference is wide.

First, the *onus* lies on you to prove that, when the goods were bought,
She had separate estate ; or else your action comes to naught.[2]

---

[1] Stat. 45 & 46 Vict. c. 75, s. 1, sub-s. 2.

[2] The Act enables married women to contract in respect of their separate property ; wherefore it was held that, in an action against a wife on her contract, the plaintiff must prove that she had separate property at the time when she made the contract ; *Palliser*

Should the wife from alienation have been thoughtfully restrained,

Though you trusted her for thousands, not a *sou* can be regained;

And, however large her income, it is equitably held

That to satisfy the smallest claim she cannot be compelled.[3]

Wives are not as single women or as men : their plight is better ;

For a wife, unless a trader, cannot make herself a debtor.

She shall not be sent to prison, like a spinster or a man,

If she will not pay her judgment creditors, although she can.[4]

She shall not be made a bankrupt (as may widow, maid, and male) ;

That is, not unless she carry on a separate trade, and fail.[5]

---

v. *Gurney*, 19 Q. B. D. 519; *Whitaker* v. *Van der Smissen*, 4 Times L. R. 707. But alas ! this fairest flower of construction hath now been ruthlessly uprooted. For an Act of 1893 provides that a wife's contract shall be deemed to be made with respect to and to bind her separate property, whether she be possessed of any separate property at the time of making the contract or not. Stat. 56 & 57 Vict. c. 63, s. 1.

[3] If a wife were entitled to separate estate under a settlement by which she was restrained from anticipating the income thereof, courts of equity would not permit it to be applied in satisfaction of her general engagements; and the Act does not interfere with this effect of a restraint on alienation ; so that a wife, so restrained, may spend her income gaily, for she shall not be compelled to pay her bills. See *Pike* v. *Fitzgibbon*, 17 Ch. D. 454 ; *Scott* v. *Morley*, 20 Q. B. D. 120, 132.

[4] Common debtors, who can pay and will not pay their debts for which their creditors have got judgment against them, may be sentenced to a term of not more than six weeks' imprisonment under the Debtors Act, 1869. It is held that a wife's contracts bind her separate property only, and cannot result in a debt which she is personally liable to pay ; hence her immunity from imprisonment for debt. *Scott* v. *Morley, ubi sup.*

[5] *Re Gardiner, Ex parte Coulson*, 20 Q. B. D. 249.

Wherefore bless, ye wives, the freedom which to you the Act accords!
Bless the Parliamentary draftsman! Bless the Commons! Bless the Lords!

Bless the judges, to whose wit ye owe the statute's explanation![6]
Bless Lord Thurlow for the clause restraining wives' anticipation![7]

Nor omit to bless the writer, who has given his spare time
To expounding married women's privilege in simple rhyme!

---

[6] *Scilicet*, Lord Esher, M.R., Lindley, Bowen, Fry, and Lopes, L.JJ., and Cave, J.
[7] According to Lord Eldon it was Lord Thurlow who first devised a clause restraining anticipation of income for insertion in a settlement securing property in trust for a wife's separate use. See 9 Ves. 404.

The Exiled Barrister's Lament.

How thickly Fate's dull jests are hurled!
How oft in our disastrous world
By circumstances man gets purled!

Such plight is mine; because I'm ill,
I am removed against my will
From my professional treadmill.

Robbed of my wonted occupation,
Condemned to rest and relaxation,
I gauge the depths of desolation.

My state of mind would find too terse
Expression in Ernulphus' curse.
No vent is adequate but verse.

Whose faith is briefly, Equity,
Whose hope is "Heaven's Chancery,"
What place for him is Italy?

The land where Nature's beauty reigns,
Where Art-enthusiasm enchains,
And compensates for lack of drains.

A barrister, who in the race
For practice hopes to win a place,
Must all æsthetic longings chase.

'Tis his ideal to find in life
No pleasure save the suitor's strife,
Have no diversion but his wife.

All meaner studies to disdain,
Devote to law alone his brain,
And struggle ceaselessly for gain.

Then since I've given all my heart
To my profession, why what part
Have I with Nature, or with Art?

How can Italian landscape please me?
How can its contemplation ease me?
And how can its enchantment seize me?

One, who must aim to be uncouth,
Should shrink from studying, in sooth,
Beauty, simplicity, and truth.

What though I'm privileged to see
The Venus dei Medici—
What lesson can it have for me?

A well-trained English legal mind
Ought to be resolutely blind
To symmetry of every kind.

It needs all man's philosophy
To bear with equanimity
The pointless jokes of Destiny !

This most of all my patience tries,
For mental solace health denies
The only literature I prize.

How can I, far from all the Courts,
Worthily occupy my thoughts
When I'm tabooed the Law Reports !

'Tis harder than I can explain,
To miss the literary gain
Their lordships' judgments all contain.

What prompts each judge to leave his traces
In observations on the cases?
And what dictates decision's bases?

I'm puzzled to embody it
In an expression apt and fit.
Can it be wisdom ?   Is it wit ?

I think I've said enough to prove
That none such sympathy should move
As one who's forced from out his groove.

Should health return, then farewell ease !
And back to work across the seas,
To briefs and consequential fees.

Should mortal sickness strike me down,
Then wrap me in my wig and gown,
    And lay my bands upon my breast ;

And reverently place my feet
Towards the Courts in Carey Street.[1]
    So let me take my last long rest !

---

[1] For members of the Honourable Society of Lincoln's Inn, who have the right of audience there, the Royal Courts of Justice are situate in Carey Street, though for suitors and other common persons, who are commanded to appear there by writs or summonses, they are said to be in the Strand.

On Husbands' Liability on their Wives' Contracts.
(1888.)

There's a theme of thrilling interest; it touches tradesmen's tills :
If a wife buy goods on credit, must her husband pay her bills?

If to sue a married woman be a perilous proceeding,[1]
How shall payment be exacted for her dressing or her feeding?

Learn the law, alarmed purveyors, lest the ladies let you in !
Listen to the legal lyrist lingering in Lincoln's Inn.

Man, to woman fast united by the matrimonial tie,
Need not pay for aught but what he authorized his wife to buy.

Man and wife together dwelling, there arises a presumption
That the wife may pledge his credit for the needful home consumption.

So in suing him for necessaries suited to their station,
Plaintiff need but prove the debt, the marriage, and cohabitation.

But imagine not that plaintiff is with legal favour glutted !
This presumption of the woman's agency may be rebutted.

---

[1] See above, p. 7, "The Married Women's Property Act, 1882, partly re-drawn."

Were the wife with needful goods, or cash to buy the same, supplied ;
If authority to pledge the husband's credit were denied ;

Then on proof of one of these alternatives (the case is hard),
The unhappy plaintiff's action is effectually barred.

If the husband for the purchase gave authority express,
Or held out the wife as agent, there the tradesman gets redress.

(You hold out your wife as agent, if you weakly pay her bills :
The judicious married reader will henceforth avoid such ills.)

Now of husband's liability when parted from his wife,
At the call of work or pleasure, or through lamentable strife,

If he wantonly desert her, turn her out into the street,
Or by harshness make her leave him, it were tedious to treat.

'Tis in " Williams' Personal " exhaustively expounded,
Where are given the authorities on which my text is grounded.[2]

So farewell, O prudent purchaser, whoever you may be !
You have counsel his opinion for a simple penny fee ![3]

---

[2] See Williams on Personal Property, pp. 495—499, 14th ed.
[3] Originally printed in the *St. James's Gazette*, price one penny.

The Case of "The Memnon."

(In the Court of Appeal, April 26, 1888, reported 4 Times Law
Reports, 501.)

Ye other
ship ye
San Salvador.

S.W.

E. by N. ½ N.
Ye Memnon.

The *Memnon* steamed in the early morn,
    Heading East-by-North half North;
They kept good watch ('twas before the dawn)
    And the look-out man peered forth.

He saw the green light of a steamship burn—
    She was heading along Sou'-West:
She will pass well under *The Memnon's* stern,
    So *The Memnon's* officer guessed.

So he kept on his course, for he made no doubt
    That the other ship would have ported;
But her watch were keeping a bad look-out,[1]
    And their view of the facts was distorted.

And her master's mind, whatever he thought,
    Some misconception harboured;
He ought to have put the helm a-port,[2]
    But he put it hard-a-starboard.

---

[1] So it is stated in the Report.
[2] So said Lord Esher in his judgment.

So his ship bore down on *The Memnon's* side,
    Which could not escape collision ;
And the question of damages came to be tried
    In the Admiralty Division.

" I must blame ye alike, however loth,"
    Said Justice Butt ; "and the sum
Of the loss incurred must be shared by both "—
    (*Judicium rusticum*).[3]

The Memnon's owners lodged an appeal !
    It was not a lucky stroke ;
And it brought on their heads more woe than weal ;
    For thus Lord Esher spoke :—

" The question is, Who is to make amends
    For this lamentable disaster ?
We have asked the advice of our nautical friends [4]
    On the acts of *The Memnon's* master.

" They say that, apart from the rules—in fact,
    From a seaman's point of view—
To his skill or caution nothing lacked,
    And he did what was best to do.

---

[3] In Courts of Admiralty jurisdiction, under a rough working rule, commonly called *judicium rusticum*, the loss is equally divided in cases of collision where both ships are found to have been in fault. Pollock on Torts, 385, 386.

[4] *Scilicet*, the nautical assessors.

" Our assessors say what he did was best ;
  But it might as well have been worst,
For whether he followed the Act is the test,
  And he ought to have slacked or reversed.[5]

"I am bound to read the Act as it stands,[6]
  And not with a grain of salt.
There was no neglect of master or hands:
  But I hold the ship in fault."

And the other judges held the same,
  Expressing polite regret.
So *The Memnon* was pronounced to blame,[7]
  And her owners' hopes upset.

But there fell from Lord Justice Lindley's lips
  These words of discontent :
" This comes of navigating ships
  By Act of Parliament !"

---

[5] By Rule 18 of the Regulations for Preventing Collision at Sea, every steamship when approaching another ship so as to involve risk of collision shall slacken her speed, or stop and reverse, if necessary.

[6] It was held in the case of *The Khedive*, 5 App. Cas. 876, that the Regulations for Preventing Collision at Sea must be strictly followed.

[7] The appeal of *The Memnon's* owners was dismissed, and Mr. Justice Butt's decision affirmed.

The Marriage Contract.

I took you for better, I took you for worse,
    For richer, for poorer, in sickness, in health ;
I was moved thereto by the length of your purse,
    And I bartered my beauty against your wealth.

Now your wealth is gone, and my beauty has paled,
    And our marriage is only a source of grief.
But, although the consideration has failed,
    A Court of Law can give no relief.

You may get off the bargain when goods are sold,
    And you—the buyer—have been deceived.
Say, new oats are sent when you wanted old,
    And you swear you *said* " old," and your word's believed.[1]

But here both the beauty and wealth were passed ;
    So I fear that reasoning won't apply :
For to promise that money or looks should last
    Would be a collateral warranty.

---

[1] See *Smith* v. *Hughes*, L. R. 6 Q. B. 597, where, however, the Court were inclined to doubt the truth of the buyer's evidence.

And consent to be joined for better, for worse,
    Through plenty or want by a life-long tie,
Implies no warranty (quite the reverse)
    That beauty or wealth should endure till we die.

So our venture has failed, and there's no redress ;
    And we point a moral, my man and I—
Don't marry for money—'Tis recklessness
    To wed for the beauty that charms the eye !

Leake v. Driffield.

(Reported 6 Times Law Reports, 35; 24 Q. B. D. 98.)

(1889.)

There is hope held out to tradesmen by a memorable Act,[1]
That a wife is, like her husband, bound to pay if she contract.

But on studying the statute, as expounded by decision,[2]
You will find that hope of payment fades away, as doth a vision.

If you sue a wife in contract, as has previously been shown,[3]
You must prove that when she bargained she had something of her own.

And her bargain is not sanctioned by a legal obligation,
If you prove she had an income—with restraint on alienation.

Mrs. D. had no effects except her wardrobe, when she bought
Goods of Leake, who promptly sued her for the price in County Court.

Judgment went against the lady, spite of reasons not a few,
Ably set forth by her counsel; for the Judge expressed this view:

---

[1] The Married Women's Property Act, 1882.

[2] See *Palliser* v. *Gurney*, 19 Q. B. D. 519; *Scott* v. *Morley*, 20 Q. B. D. 120; and consider the present case.

[3] See above, p. 15, "The Married Women's Property Act, 1882, partly re-drawn." And see from the note there made how our legislature hath unchivalrously changed the law, and snatched away from the married woman's diadem one of the choicest of her gems.

"She had separate estate within the meaning of the Act ;
In respect of her apparel she was able to contract."

To a contrary opinion does a woman ever yield ?
Does a wife brook opposition ?   Mrs. D. at once appealed.

Said the Judges,[4] "It afflicts us with unutterable woe
To reverse our little brother[5] in the County Court below ;

"But, as Judges, we are bound to give decision, independent
Of our feelings, and we here must enter judgment for defendant.

"It's a notion common sense abhors, judicial reason loathes,
That a wife should make a contract on the credit of her clothes !

"We have heard that if a gambler coin of legal tender lack,
He will bet his boots, or lay the very shirt upon his back.

"But we cannot think that any wife would pledge her 'combination'[6]
As security that just demands shall meet with liquidation.

"So we hold that married women who have nothing but their raiment,
If they purport to contract, can never be compelled to payment."

---

[4] Mathew, J., and Wills, J.
[5] A judge of County Courts is of inferior dignity to a judge of the High Court ; yet may they be said to be in a manner brethren.
[6] *Scilicet*, the combination garment.

Passing Reflections on Admiralty Law.

(Suggested by the Case of *The Vindomora*, 14 P. D. 172.)

Oh! the mariner carries his life in his hand;
  Of wind or of weather he recks not a pea;
But he quails at the thought of the judges on land,
  And the Rules for Preventing Collisions at Sea!

For he may not rely on his nautical skill
  To save the good ship he commands from collision;
Mere seamanship will not preserve him from ill,
  If he counter the Rules as explained by decision.[1]

So when danger approaches the seafaring man,
  And his plight demands promptitude, nerve, and decision,
Before he can act he must carefully scan
  The latest reports of the " Probate [2] Division."

---

[1] It has been held that the rules for preventing collisions at sea have the force of an Act of Parliament, and must be strictly obeyed (*The Khedive*, 5 App. Cas. 501); and a ship will not be excused from blame, in a case of collision, if her master disobey the rules, even though the nautical assessors advise that what was done was the best thing for him to do. (See the case of *The Memnon*, p. 25, above.)

[2] Admiralty cases are reported along with Probate and Divorce cases in a volume cited as " Probate Division."

Far stranger than fiction is that which is true!
    (To a cynical mind the idea is a high jest)
When a moment's delay may destroy ship and crew,
    The captain must sit down and study the Digest.[3]

A sea-lawyer's a type that has not a good name;
    He's a sort of canary-bird not worth his groundsel!
But the skipper, whose object is freedom from blame,
    Had best give no order not settled by counsel.

Though the Rules must be followed, 'tis pleasant to feel
    That the law is asserted with due moderation;
And the master (so held by the Court of Appeal[4])
    May at times have a hand in the ship's navigation.

In a case of collision, 'twas put to the Court,
    That the captains of vessels by law are forbidden
To change the direction to starboard or port
    When the fog is so dense that all objects are hidden.[5]

The contention of counsel was patiently heard
    By the Judges, who said: " You have argued with force;
But to lay down a hard and fast rule is absurd,
    That a ship in a fog may not alter her course."

Wherefore, mariners bold, be no longer distraught,
    Let no dread Regulation your courage o'erwhelm!
For no absolute rule is laid down by the Court
    That a ship in a fog may not alter her helm!

---

[3] To wit, Pritchard's Admiralty Digest (these are bulky tomes), and the other Digests of Admiralty cases. Without these works the equipment of a practical seaman is incomplete.

[4] See the case of *The Vindomora*, 14 P. D. 172.

[5] See the argument of Sir W. Phillimore and Mr. J. P. Aspinall in the last-mentioned case.

Of Fraudulent Brokers and Outraged Bankers.
(1890.)

By the common law 'tis settled, he who parts with goods for pelf,
Can transfer no better title than the right he has himself;

Though if goods in market overt be notoriously sold,
These against the very owner buyers have the right to hold.

Save that if the goods in question were unlawfully obtained,
Then the unoffending purchaser may forfeit what he gained;

For the owner of such chattels gets by statute this relief,
That to him reverts the title on conviction of the thief.

But to cash and notes, that pass from hand to hand like money bright,
Taken in good faith for value, law annexes valid right.

And of this exception there are now included in the range
All securities negotiable upon the Stock Exchange.

There's a custom in the City, whereby brokers borrow money
From the bankers lending gladly, keen as bees to gather honey;

And the brokers (gentle reader, it may give your mind a shock)
Pledge securities—their own and those of others too—*en bloc.*

And the bankers ask no questions ; though, as has been plainly shown,[1]
They are well aware that brokers' pledges are not all their own.

Now suppose, without authority, a broker pledges bonds
Which are not his, but his client's, then is bankrupt, or absconds ;

For solution by the Court a knotty point of law is set—
Can the banks retain the client's bonds against the broker's debt ?

And the Courts of Law have held that, as the banks which made the loan,
Knowing all they took in mortgage not to be the broker's own,

Yet with adequate inquiry thought it proper to dispense,
Purchase in good faith for value shall not serve as their defence.

There is wailing in the City.   All the bankers there are frantic ;
They incontinently stigmatize the judges as pedantic.

And they call upon their deity (the golden calf), " How long
Shall our business be infected with this plague of right and wrong ?"[2]

With what harassing restrictions is the banker's calling hedged,
If he cannot make advances on things fraudulently pledged !

---

[1] See *Lord Sheffield v. London Joint Stock Bank*, 13 App. Cas. 333; *Simmons v. London Joint Stock Bank*, 6 Times L. R. 243.

[2] And apparently their prayer was heard, for the case here celebrated was reversed on appeal to the House of Lords, and the previous decision of the same august tribunal in *Lord Sheffield v. London Joint Stock Bank* was criticised with thinly-veiled contempt. See *London Joint Stock Bank v. Simmons*, [1892] A. C. 201.

Beatæ Possidentes, quas Lex non cogit ad Solutionem.
(1891.)

Listen, listen, honoured ladies, by the law's unbending rigour
Banned from Parliament and Council, 'spite your intellectual vigour,

Come and taste of consolation in the happy situation
Of the wife, who has an income, with restraint on alienation.

For a woman with a husband (best of all Dame Fortune's prizes)
Modern law, austere to others, has a store of sweet surprises.

Thus, if anxious to secure her ardent nature's free expansion,
She may fearlessly abandon the marital couch and mansion.

She may snap her dainty fingers at the conjugal petition
For the rights, of which Lord Esher failed to find a definition.[1]

True, the wife may be decreed to pay a yearly compensation
To the husband, whom she lightly leaves to married isolation.

That is, if she own unfettered wealth, or earn in humble station;
Not if, blessed with worldly goods, she be denied anticipation.

---

[1] See *R.* v. *Jackson*, [1891] 1 Q. B. 671.

For, provided with an income, but restrained from alienation,
She cannot be made to pay towards her consort's sustentation.[2]

Such a wife, 'tis wisely settled by our lawgivers far-seeing,
Shall fulfil in peace the mission of her own poetic being.

Tradesmen will supply on credit all her wants of food and raiment;
Yet shall every base purveyor sue her fruitlessly for payment.

Now I rede ye right, fair ladies, ye must heed a small condition,
If ye wish to rest secure in unassailable position.

It is easy to comply with; it is merely that you must
Be bereft of ready money when you order goods on trust.

Simply follow what I tell you (for you need not understand).
It is dangerous to go on tick with money left in hand;

Since unsympathetic judges (who they are, I shall not mention)
Will be eager to impute to you contractual intention.[3]

But you need not fear their judgment, I, the legal bard have said it,
If you only spend your income first, then order goods on credit.

Surely e'en the host angelic can afford no happier station,
Than the wife's, who has an income, with restraint on alienation!

---

[2] Under the Act of 1884, which abolished imprisonment for contempt of a decree for restitution of conjugal rights, a wife refusing to return to her husband may be decreed to make a settlement on him out of her property or earnings; but not, it has been held, out of any property which she is restrained from anticipating. *Mitchell* v. *Mitchell*, [1891] P. 203.

[3] Judges have been found to presume that a lady intended to make herself liable to pay for many pounds worth of goods, though she had but a few shillings in hand. See *Everitt* v. *Paxton*, 7 Times L. R. 465. Now, as we have seen, the law doth impute contractual intention to wives, though they have nothing. See above, p. 16.

After Writing of Contingent Remainders.

I have gravely considered the learning,
　　I have solemnly cited Lord Coke,
I have sternly resisted the yearning
　　To treat the whole thing as a joke.
Now my effort to teach the young draftsman
　　Is soberly set down in ink,
Let me cast off the cant of the craftsman,
　　And say what I think !

With a progeny littered in fractions
　　Is our old Father Antic[1] accurst ;
But of all his amorphous abstractions
　　A contingent remainder's the worst !
'Tis a featureless fantasy, founded
　　On a vile metaphorical rule,[2]
In some dry-as-dust brain was it rounded.
　　Oh ! mind as of mule !

---

[1] " . . . . the rusty curb of old Father Antic the Law."—*Per* Sir
John Falstaff, Henry IV. Pt. I. Act 1. Sc. 2.
[2] Namely, that every contingent remainder must have a particular
estate of freehold to support it.

Who devised a contingent remainder,
    May remorse everlastingly gnaw !
May they suffer eternal attainder
    For polluting the old common law !
May their shades be unceasingly hooted,
    Be cast out at the point of the toe !
May their dwellings be promptly uprooted
    Wherever they go !

And to all their pedantic successors,
    Who contrive to wrest reason awry
(Set of straw-chopping palsied professors),
    May the curse of Ernulphus apply !
I would like to hang up, high as Haman,
    Every text-writer, jurist, and judge,
Who gives ground for the taunt of the layman,
    That law is all fudge !

Say the scoffers, " 'The law is a juggle,
    'Tis a trade, 'tis a specious pretence,
'Tis a trick to make costs, 'tis a struggle,
    To petrify quick common sense !"
Though I felt the fell finger of famine,
    I would never concede they are right :
But there's much it is best to examine
    In humorous light !

So I rede thee, raw youngster, who yearnest
    To learn the long legend of law,
That thou shouldst not take too much in earnest
    Every jerk of the just judge's jaw.
Let thy labours be lightened with laughter,
    Most melodious music on earth,
So thy mind shall be sound ever after,
    And mellow with mirth!

A Ballad of Lords Ailesbury and Iveagh, and the Vendor and Purchaser Act, 1874.

(See *Re Marquis of Ailesbury and Lord Iveagh*, [1893] 2 Ch. 345.

Lord Ailes-
bury selleth
land to Lord
Iveagh—

Lord Ailesbury sold his ancestral land ;
    But a tenant for life was he.
By previous deeds, ye must understand,
    It was subject to jointures three.

under the
Settled Land
Act, 1882, for
an unincum-
bered estate
in fee.

Lord Iveagh, Lord Iveagh, the power is great
    Which the statute gives to me.
I warrant I grant ye as full estate
    As though I were seised in fee.

Lord Iveagh
questioneth
the extent of
the statutory
power.

Lord Iveagh laughed, and Lord Iveagh frowned ;
    Ye may tell the marines, quoth he,
That the statute gars ye give your ground
    From the prior jointures free.

The argument
of Mr. Buck-
ley, Q.C., and
Mr. Cyprian
Williams,
[1] citing *Bruce
v. Ailesbury*,
[1892] A. C.
356.

Look, my Lord Judge, what is said in the Act,
    As openly as need be.
And, for good guidance hath not lacked,[1]
    Consider its policee !

<table>
<tr><td>Mr. Spencer Butler's argument.</td><td>

For Lord Iveagh the judge was sore besought.
   I pray thee, give heed to me!
Was never no such undoing wrought
   But and if this thing might be!

</td></tr>
</table>

<table>
<tr><td>Mr. Cyprian Williams having replied, his Lordship reserved judgment.</td><td>

Much more these counsel told the Court;
   Full well they earned their fee!
But a rhymed report must needs be short.
   Cur' vult advisari.[2]

</td></tr>
</table>

<table>
<tr><td>Judgment delivered.</td><td>

And now at last to quell the strife,
   This worthy judge quoth he,
Lord Ailesbury holds the land for life,
   Which is subject to jointures three.

But I ween it is all one settlement;
   So I deem it right that he
Shall convey the land, so is the intent,
   From every jointure free.

</td></tr>
</table>

---

[2] N.B.—You must speak this line according to the new-fangled pronunciation of Latin; the which, it is said, the Romans themselves used.

Golf.[1]

(*Villanelle.*)

I'm ten holes down and eight to play;
    I'll give up this annoying game;
I vow I'll give my clubs away.

I've topped and foozled all the way,
    I've missed the globe, and, crowning shame!
I'm ten holes down and eight to play.

Such wicked words I'm led to say,
    I risk the purgatorial flame.
I vow I'll give my clubs away.

My niblick I could lift to slay
    My caddie, though not his the blame,
I'm ten holes down and eight to play.

I'll flee from murder while I may;
    Farewell! fond dream of golfing fame!
I vow I'll give my clubs away.

---

[1] This is written, generally, of the practising barrister's golf; and
therefore it is included in this collection. And, in particular, it is
written of the poet's own golf.

I've lost my temper every day ;
    Each trivial round the luck's the same.
I'm ten holes down and eight to play ;
I vow I'll give my clubs away.

The Lay of the Lame Limitation and the Lost Inheritance.

How well it is when you mean to part
　　With chattel or land in a life-long way
To instruct one versed in the draftsman's art
　　And the technical talk of the now cold clay
Of Davidson and Dart![1]

My father settled his land by deed;
　　In the joy of wedding a fair young wife
He signed and sealed[2] a disastrous screed,
　　Which limited all to himself for life,
With a jointure for her meed.

---

[1] Davidson's Precedents in Conveyancing and Dart's Vendors and Purchasers are works of great profit and guidance to the conveyancer, so that of each learned author it may be said, He being dead yet speaketh.

[2] Note that it is the better opinion that there is no need to sign a deed as well as to seal it : but it is a good opinion that it is better to seal a deed and to sign it as well.

And after his death, the deed declares
    (My father's wishes it ill defines)[3]
That the land shall go in equal shares
    To all his children and their assigns,
But it does not say "their heirs."

Father has suffered the common fate.
    What interest do we children hold ?
Consider, counsel, and answer straight
    In his opinion, we are told,
Each has but a life estate.

"Grant to A., and he holds till life is done,
    "No longer, without you add 'and his heirs,'
"Or, 'in fee simple' since '81 ;[4]
    "Grant to A. and assigns, and alike he fares,
"As appears from Littleton.

"You were meant to take all, I suppose ;
    "But you lose the fee[5] by a probable slip.
"For words inapt your father chose
    "To confer the fullest ownership
"That the law of England knows.

---

[3] Now, if there were clear proof of this, it might be that a Court of Equity would rectify the deed : but it is like that the narrator speaketh, as is the habit of laymen, upon conjecture rather than evidence.

[4] This is by virtue of the Conveyancing Act, 1881.   The law is thus enriched with one more technicality.

[5] That is to say, the estate in fee simple, a greater estate than which a man cannot have.

" Had he mentioned ' heirs,' you had all in store,
　　" An estate ' assigns ' could not enhance.[8]
" Through a scribe unskilled in legal lore
　　" You are all despoiled of inheritance
" For want of a few words more."

Oh ! the little more, and what gain to me !
　　And the little less, and how poor I stand !
How a word may enlarge freehold to fee,[7]
　　Or its lack arrest a grant of land
At the death of the grantee !

There are queer old rules in the law of land,
　　Such as that set forth in my rugged rhymes,
Which at first no doubt were shrewdly planned,
　　But, without a knowledge of byegone times,
No fellow can understand !

---

　[8] For the words " and his assigns," added to a gift to one and his
heirs, are but indicative of the power of alienation which he would
possess without them.

　[7] He that hath an estate for life hath an estate of freehold : but an
estate of inheritance he cannot have without words of inheritance, *ut
supra.*

Companhia de Moçambique v. *British South Africa Company.*

(Reported, L. R. [1892] 2 Q. B. 358; [1893] A. C. 602.)

The State-
ment of Claim.

They have broken our close[1] with force and arms;
  They have taken our goods away;
They have beaten our servants, and caused alarms
  Of assault by night and day!
And for all these multifarious harms
  Redress as of right we pray!

The Defence.

Far, far away
  On Afric's burning shore
The *locus in quo*[2] lay;
  Remains there as before![3]

---

[1] " Every unwarrantable entry on another's soil the law entitles a trespass by *breaking his close ;* the words of the writ of trespass commanding the defendant to show cause, *quare querentis clausum fregit.* For every man's land is, in the eye of the law, enclosed and set apart from his neighbour's; and that either by a visible and material fence, as one field is divided from another by a hedge, or by an ideal invisible boundary, existing only in the contemplation of the law, as when one man's land adjoins to another's in the same field."—3 Black. Com. 209.

[2] That is to say, the place where the alleged enormous injuries were done.

[3] As Master Anthony Fitzherbert hath recorded, " *Terre demurt*

D 2

Of land that lies beyond the sea
The English Courts will hold no plea.
You cannot remedy your woes
    By any legal fiction
In trespass why we broke your close
    Outside the jurisdiction !

The Plaintiff's argument.

In days of old,
    Procedure was formal.
Judges were cold ;
    Strict rule was normal.
Trespass to land,
    By townsman or yokel,
Rigidly scanned,
    Was held to be local :[4]

---

terre tout temps, mes biens come boefs ou vache puit estre mange."—
Fitz. Abr. Villenage, pl. 22. And again, another learned lawyer hath
said, "No man, be he ever so feloniously disposed, can run away with
an acre of land." And without an asportation, or carrying away,
there can be no larceny at the common law, though one have *animum
furandi.*

[4] As the learned compiler of the immortal Leading Cases explained :—Anciently the law required that the *venue, visne* or *vicinetum,*
in other words, the neighbourhood whence juries were to be summoned,
should be also that in which the cause of action had arisen ; and the
parties litigant were required to state in their pleadings with the utmost
certainty, not merely the county, but the very *venue—i.e.,* the very dis-
trict, hundred, or vill within that county—where the facts that they
alleged had taken place. Afterwards the Courts were induced to take a
distinction between *transitory* matters, such as a contract, which might
happen anywhere, and *local* ones, such as a trespass to the realty which
could only happen in one particular place ; and they established, as a rule,

Nor would the Court
    Be cajoled by a fiction,
Counting[5] this tort,
    Done beyond jurisdiction,
As suffered in London.[6]
But all this is undone!

In modern practice
    You claim as you please.
Grateful the Act[7] is
    Which set us at ease.

---

that in *transitory* matters the plaintiff should have a right to lay the *venue* where he pleased. (1 Smith, L. C. 363, 2nd ed.; notes to *Mostyn* v. *Fabrigas*.)   And an action of trespass, *quare clausum fregit*, was held to be local in *Shelling* v. *Farmer*, 1 Str. 646, and *Doulson* v. *Matthews*, 4 T. R. 503.   So that the fraction of outlandish closes was not cognisable by the Courts.

    [5] The first pleading in an action at Common Law was the declaration, *narratio*, or *count*, anciently called the tale, in which the plaintiff set forth his cause of complaint at length : 3 Black. Comm. 293.   *Count* cometh of the French word *conte* : Co. Litt. 17a.

    [6] Transitory matters arising out of the realm could be tried in the English Courts by a fiction of law, whereby the plaintiff was allowed to declare, say, that the defendant assaulted him at Minorca (to wit) at London, in the parish of St. Mary-le-Bow, in the ward of Cheap. (*Mostyn* v. *Fabrigas, ubi sup.*)   And this case a poet hath melodiously expounded in rhyme, with a most exquisite and haunting refrain ; see Leading Cases done into English, by Sir Frederick Pollock.   And though he there said it was obsolete, yet was it oftentimes cited in the case at bar, both by counsel and by the justices and the lords; though I do not know they referred to the metrical version thereof.

    [7] The Act referred to is the Judicature Act of 1873, or, more correctly, that Act, together with the other Judicature Acts, which began

Whate'er the fact is,
     The justices seize
On the mischief made
     By the malice of man,
And administer aid
     On a liberal plan![6]

The result.

This argument failed to secure the decision
Of the Judges who sat in the Queen's Bench Division.
Then the Court of first instance's work was undone,
On the Plaintiffs' appeal, by two judges to one.
     But their moment of triumph was fleeting !
They were dragged to the Lords' House and utterly
     lost;
Both there and below they were cast in the cost ;
     And the bread of affliction they're eating !

---

in 1875. Under these Acts, the old formal pleadings have been utterly abolished, and suitors, or rather their counsel or solicitors, make instead what are called statements of claim.

[6] And indeed there is some countenance for the supposition that justice is now administered without technicality in the great multitude of rules issued by the judges to save the ill-advised from destruction. Upon which many thousand doubts and difficulties arise, and must be solved at the suitor's expense. And truly he doth sweat and grunt for our support, and out of his stony griefs we are fed !

> " *Suave, mari magno turbantibus æquora ventis*
> *E terra magnum alterius spectare laborem.*
> *Non quia vexari quemquam est jucunda voluptas,*
> *Sed, quibus ipse malis careas, quia cernere suave est.*"

" Our procedure was amended

    " By the Judicature Acts,

" Counts[9] at common law are ended ;

    " Claims should simply state the facts.

" But relief is not extended

    " To encompass a transaction

" Never previously commended

    " As a legal cause of action."

---

[9] Of counts, see above, p. 53.

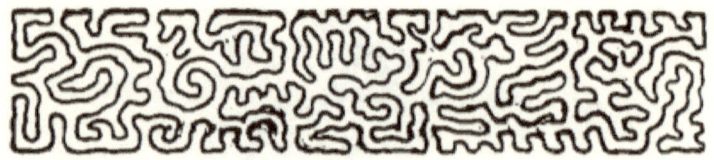

Mighell v. Sultan of Johore.

(Reported, 10 Times Law Reports, 37, 115; L. R. [1894] 1 Q. B. 149.)

Jenny Mighell brought an action 'gainst the Sultan of Johore,
And demanded satisfaction for the maiden name she bore.

She declared, as Albert Baker, he had wooed her for his bride,
But he now declined to take her to be consort at his side.

Quoth the Sultan, " Such divinity doth hedge about a King,
" That (although there's nothing in it) I need not deny the thing.

" Be it fact or be it fiction that I scrupled not to fool her,
" This Court hath not jurisdiction o'er an independent ruler."

Said the Judge, " Your plea has met the plaintiff's case, I don't deny :
" But your royal *status* let the Foreign Office certify."

From a Foreign Office clerk a note was sent to say what store
There is set by Abubakar, Maharajah of Johore.

" He's a *bonâ fide* sovereign, our gracious Queen's ally,
" Reigning independent of her and of any feudal tie.

" He has land and naval forces, postal system, and a Court,
" Where his delegate discourses law of contract, crime, and tort.

" He has founded orders knightly ; titles, honours, he bestows.
" So remaining yours politely, this epistle here I close."

Then the Judges, after reading the above precise report,
Held that Abubakar's pleading put the plaintiff out of Court.

" Say, that like Haroun Al Rasched, he preferred to walk unknown ;
" Say, the hapless maid was mashéd by his princely form and tone.

" Say, he offered lawful wedlock: still he never made submission
" To be sued (and that's the deadlock) for his promise's rescission.

" By the comity of nations, legal process won't intrude
" On men holding kingly stations ; they're exempt from being sued.

" As to this, law, reason's flower, does not differentiate
" A great European power from a petty potentate."

Now a bard of light and leading has bewailed the lost delight
Of the ancient subtle pleading[1] gone into *die Ewigkeit.*

---

[1]
    " Sing sorrow for money had and received,
     And alack for the common counts, O."
        Per Sir F. Pollock in Leading Cases done into English,
             Marriott v. *Hampton.*
The which, he saith, doth express in very lamentable wise the author's grief and heavi-
ness at the downfall of Pleading.

I would beg him mark, to ease him of his sorrow, what I pen
(Sure it cannot fail to please him, and all legal-minded men) :

That the law we yet inherit[2] lets an action, as we see,
Be dismissed, apart from merit, on a dilatory plea!

---

[2] *Inherit.* Note that it is regularly true, as hath been said elsewhere, that English law is an Englishman's best inheritance. Yet hath law been likened unto the inheritance of an everlasting disease :—

> "*Es erben sich Gesetz' und Rechte*
> *Wie eine ew'ge Krankheit fort.*"
> *Per* Mephistopheles in Goethe's Faust.

But mark, reader, first, that the poet doth here put this speech into the mouth of the foul fiend himself, the enemy of mankind, who is to utter this enormous scandal and libel to the confounding of a silly scholar. Secondly, it doth not appear that this was spoken of the English common law, which hath ever been upheld for the perfection of reason : but it seemeth rather to be alleged of the Imperial Law of Rome, or it may be, of the provincial customs of the Germans, or again, it may be, of the sacred Canons and Constitutions of the Church. Thirdly, neither the poet, nor his puppet, the Devil, was ever of counsel learned in the law, as the writer is ; and therefore their word can have no weight nor authority. And I tell thee, my son, that if there were given unto thee the wisdom of all the philosophers and poets, this should not avail thee to deliver a good opinion upon a point of law, without thou wert learned in the books wherein are recorded the debating, doubting and determination of the justices upon the questions argued before them.

FINIS.